Elias Colbert

Scoriæ

Eulogy on Shakespeare (1864) - What we breathe (1869) - The first

Christmas-eve (1874) - The sun that never sets (1879)

Elias Colbert

Scoriæ
*Eulogy on Shakespeare (1864) - What we breathe (1869) - The first Christmas-eve
(1874) - The sun that never sets (1879)*

ISBN/EAN: 9783337380854

Printed in Europe, USA, Canada, Australia, Japan

Cover: Foto ©Andreas Hilbeck / pixelio.de

More available books at **www.hansebooks.com**

SCORIÆ.

EULOGY ON SHAKESPEARE.
(1864)

WHAT WE BREATHE.
(1869)

THE FIRST CHRISTMAS-EVE.
(1874)

THE SUN THAT NEVER SETS.
(1879)

By ELIAS COLBERT, M.A.

CHICAGO:
FERGUS PRINTING COMPANY.
1883.

THE Eulogy on Shakespeare was pronounced (by Evelyn Evans) in Bryan Hall, Chicago, April 23, 1864; at the Tercentenary celebration of the poet's birthday. As it has been submitted to a Procrustean process, for publication in the "Analytical Sixth Reader" and "The American Elocutionist," I consider myself justified in reproducing it, entire, for private circulation.

It is due to the truth of history to say that the Eulogy was written "on the spur of the moment"; at the request of a committee from the St. George's Society, who discovered, only two night's before the celebration, that the task had been neglected by a gentleman to whom it was originally assigned. I have preferred *not* to make a few changes, suggested during a more leisurely perusal.

The "First Christmas Eve" was written under less pressure for time; which, to the work of the journalist is not always an advantage. It was published in the "Tribune," of December 24, 1874.

"What We Breathe" is copied from the "American Builder", for April, 1870; but, as a matter of authorship, nearly all of it belongs to the work of the year 1869.

"The Sun that Never Sets" was prepared in response to a toast assigned to me on the occasion of celebrating Washington's Birthday, at the University of Chicago, in 1879. As the hall was too dark to permit reading, the "points" of the paper were not all brought out; and the astronomical class of that epoch did not know how little it missed for want of more light on a dark subject.

These articles are diversions from the prosaic routine of the commercial department of a newspaper, and the still graver logic of "celestial mechanics". If not deemed worthy to be called "pearls of thought", they may perhaps take rank with the Gracchi, who, it will be remembered, were Cornelians. If not that, then the reader may fall back on my own designation; and class them as scoriæ.

E. C.

Chicago, May 1, 1883.

SHAKESPEARE.

1564-1864.

————

THREE hundred years ago to-day was born in an obscure village in the middle of England one who, though boasting no honorable birth, was destined to shine as the sun in the literary firmament — William Shakespeare, the Bard of Avon. History does not state that an eagle hovered around his infantile head, or that he strangled a serpent at his birth. He was a common looking child, with common surroundings. This, and nothing more.

Neither in his boyhood do we witness the exhibition of any of those feats of intellectual prowess with the record of which historians delight to deck the monuments of departed heroes. We read of no prodigies of childish acquirement, no precocity of intellect;—not even of that strange and wondrous leaning and longing after the beautiful, which is usually dignified with the name of juvenile genius. None of this; and opportunities for the development

of the latent talent within him were few indeed.
He received but a common-school education at
the free-school in Stratford, which in those days
meant—we can not say how little. Even that
was soon concluded through family misfortune.
Nor in his adolescence did he give audible
promise of that sunlight of intellect which was
destined to flood the whole earth with its rays,
through all coming time.

As was the boy, so was the young man : giv-
ing no sign of future greatness, save in the pos-
session of that free, fearless spirit of adventure
which is the true type of Nature's nobleman—
he who disdains the petty conventionalities and
repudiates the trammeling formulas of society.
He surrounded himself with family ties at the
early age of eighteen; and even in that ad-
vanced stage of existence we recognize only the
spirit of a man which, like the young eagle,
wastes not its strength in petty circling flights
ere its pinions are grown, but remains unseen by
the other denizens of the air till it has attained
the power to soar heavenward amid the bright
effulgence, almost at the first essay, leaving all
others far away in the ignoble depths below.

His earlier life is nothing save as a prelude to
the coming man. His boisterous sportings, his
carousals, his experience as tutor even, are as
naught. In his deer-stealing experience we
first see the germ of poetic talent; and to that

act of indiscretion we are indebted, probably, for all worth knowing. That flight to London at the age of twenty-three, to escape the wrath of a Lucy—ignoble as it was—proved to be the road to his usefulness and renown. How shall we trace him thereafter, through the successive occupations of call-boy, minor actor, writer, and leader, till he became the bosom friend of earth's noblest minds, among whom he shone as the sun among stars—the man before whose amazing intellectual wealth all who knew him bowed in reverential homage?

We can not follow his history chronologically; it is only as the *natural* historian counts developments and compares phases of existence that we can hope to study him. The lapse of less than three short centuries has enveloped in the cloud of tradition all that pertains to his personal career. Yet these clouds are only as the fog on the horizon. Above that bound rises majestically the orb of light—the one central mind, which, like the god of day, sends forth scintillations, innumerable and eternally enduring. Scarce a breath of vapor obscures the view. The difficulty, if any, lies only in ourselves, as unable to bear the effulgent plenitude of his beams, we blink and gaze, and turn and look again, till almost blinded with the effort. See him as he darts forth his rays of purest light, illumining the dark and hitherto

undiscovered recesses of the human heart, bringing into full play the affections and passions,
and powers of his characters, and opening up to
us a mine of rich treasures, sparkling and flash-
ing like the blaze of diamonds, where before we
only saw the dim shadowy outline of its form.
Watch him as with true pantomimic power he
exposes to view all the variations of human
thought, and action; and with kaleidoscopic
versatility changes from scene to scene, from
object to object, till we are bewildered with the
effect, and feel—if not intoxicated like the
opium reveller—yet as if the tree of the knowledge of good and evil had shed its fruit for us,
and we had eaten and become truly wise!

In this one trait lies the peculiar, the omnipo-
tential power of Shakespeare. He does not
attempt to create character, but to unfold it.
He aims not to give to the world that which
was *not*, but to reveal that which was and *is* and
ever shall be. He sought not the vain glory of
a Faust who was swallowed up by his own creation, but to hold the mirror to already-existing
nature, to give herself undisguisedly, nothing
extenuating nor setting down aught in malice; to
present the image of the things themselves, and
edify or amuse only by their comparisons or
contrasts. Beyond this he had no ambition, he
soared not after the illimitable, or even the diffi-
cult; his situations are all possible, his actions

natural; the substantive is presented first, then the verb; the accessories are applied judiciously, never with a too lavish hand.

It is of the heart that Shakespeare speaks; he probes to its inmost recesses, and lays bare its most hidden workings. The subterfuges of the hypocrite are like plastic clay in his hands. At "one fell swoop" he dives deep and brings to the surface the leading trait, which there fixed is surrounded by its necessary adjuncts only. In each of his personalities one sees the innate character—the primary motive of action; it shines out in every word, defying concealment. Neither are they elaborated so as to be wearisome. One touch, and the image is before you, not a thousand labored words, but one bold, truth-speaking line brings out in full relief all one needs to know. Another and another is treated with equal skill. Almost in the twinkling of an eye, the panorama is before you. Its parts all separately introduced; yet so rapidly, and so skilfully blended, as to give the idea of complete, perfect oneness.

As he speaks of the heart, so he speaks *to* the heart. His portrayals are things of life—speaking likenesses. We appreciate them instantaneously. Not that it is given to any one man in any age to comprehend the inexhaustible variety of character to be found in his works, but that all not beyond our experience, and

therefore above appreciation, is instantly recognized as a perfect personation. Hence the
varying estimation in which Shakespeare is held.
The most unlettered boor is melted to tears or
carried away in raptures at a proper rendition
of his characters, because there is a language of
the heart which needs no learning to enable us
to interpret. But he comprehends not all.
The more exquisite touches, the blendings of
the natural with the artificial, are only to be
duly appreciated as we rise in our knowledge of
humanity. Our horizon is limited thus by what
we know; but never yet has one attained to
that elevation whence he could look down and
beyond the confines of Shakesperian thought.
He who knows most has always venerated the
Bard most highly; and inasmuch as the heart of
man is substantially the same in all ages and
under all conditions, variable only in its mani-
festations, the perfectly truthful is always recog-
nizable under the shifting shams of civilized
advancement. That which is true in one age is
true in all; and the characters of Shakespeare
will never die, never grow antiquated, but
always retain the vigor and freshness of the
Elizabethian age, so long as humanity itself
endures.

This plentitude is now so universally acknowl-
edged, that criticisms are justly regarded as odi-
ous. To tell how well or how badly Shake-

speare wrote, to attempt to institute a standard
of judgment, is just so much as to essay the
determination of absolute brightness in the
solar ray—it is rather the standard of perfection
to which, as to a touchstone, we refer all else.
We say "Shakespeare wrote," and we say "The
sun shines." The want of appreciation in either
case lies not with them but with us—the clouds
that obscure the car of Apollo are of earthly
origin; beyond them the sun always shines
bright, serene, clear, beautiful, perfect.

The natal day of Shakespeare is also the day
of St. George. While Englishmen may feel
justly proud of his fame, they are only his more
immediate neighbors. The whole world claims
kin. A perfect cosmopolite in thought, he had
made the learning of other peoples his own; he
was equally at home in delineating the special-
ties of men of foreign birth as of those who
drew their first breath on his native soil.

Two hundred and forty-eight years have
passed since the great one departed. He still
lives—his memory shall never die. Far as the
wide range of civilization extends, his works are
read. The Hindoo and the Laplander, equally
with ourselves, appreciate them. In his writ-
ings, the great Shakespeare flourishes in immortal youth. When the conquerors of earth shall
have been forgotten, he who opened up a new
universe of thought shall be cherished in the

memories of a grateful world.   Each succeeding age does him greater homage; and when
man shall have attained to the highest possible
perfection of intellectual culture, then, and then
only, will the value of the services which he ren-
dered to humanity be really appreciated.   The
noble thoughts to which he first gave expres-
sion will form the axiomata of future ages, and
their purifying, elevating, ennobling influence,
will largely tend to bring about that for which
all men pray—the good time coming.   Then,
and then only will his eulogium be written;
then only will the world know how largely it
has been indebted to William Shakespeare.

WHAT WE BREATHE.

1869-70.

In the January number of THE BUILDER we published a few facts in relation to the suspension of common salt in the atmosphere, and its distribution over the whole earth's surface. Our statement was that the quantity of salt taken up from the ocean annually is equal to a layer of one-sixteenth of an inch in thickness, spread over land and sea. But salt is only one among thousands of substances which the winds lick up as they flit along; and carry about, to be deposited in some distant quarter.

We are all familiar with the fact that a strong wind raises clouds of dust; but few of us stop to consider of how many different forms of matter that dust is composed, or how much of it is continually held up from the bosom of mother earth, even in the calmest day. To appreciate the first, we must remember that not only are earth and stones pulverized by passing wheels in the street, but that disintegration is an inevitable concomitant of existence. We construct a monument of the hardest marble, and the tooth of time eats into it remorsely till it crumbles away, and the deepest inscription is eventually effaced. The iron column rusts away, and wooden furniture decays and mildews, even when shut up in a still room. The iron tires, and the shoes of man or horse, which pulverize the stone or grind up the wooden pavement in traveling, are themselves rubbed away in the process, and require constant renewal. The pores of the skin give forth a continuous perspiration, and from the breathing organs of men and animals a never-ceasing stream of gaseous impurity is poured forth into the air, bearing with it myriads of solid particles which are no longer needed in the system. And as with the animal, so with the vegetable world. The pollen of the growing flower, and the fully-formed seed, are carried off on the wings of the wind; the withering leaves are blown hither and thither, and pulverized till their constituent particles are fit to be borne aloft in the ærial flight; and the plant itself follows in the same endless procession, after it has fulfilled its allotted individual mission.

"Dust thou art, and unto dust thou shalt return," was a part of the original sentence; but its application is not limited to man; it applies to all created things. Even the waters of the ocean become dust, after having been evaporated, and sent down from the clouds to form part of the structure of plant and animal. Alike from the granite rock, and the fluttering wing of the insect, the winds continually sweep off minute particles of matter, reducing the former in size, and requiring the incessant formation of new vitalized structure to keep up the bulk of the latter. All forms, animate and inanimate, alike turn to dust.

We may gain a faint idea of the enormous quantities of this mingled detritus of animal, vegetable, and mineral matter, which are normally contained in the atmosphere, by a little investigation. The hardest glass is scratched by much rubbing, though with the finest handkerchief—a fact which astronomers recognize, and rub the glasses of their telescopes as little as possible. In this case, it is not the fibre of the handkerchief which scratches, but the minute particles of dust that float in the atmosphere till they become entangled in the filaments of the cambric. Look at a sunbeam as it comes through the window: you see millions of atoms dancing about in it. There are just as many atoms of dust in the same number of cubic inches of atmosphere in any other part of the room, and we fail to see them only because they are not contrastively illuminated. Professor Tyndall has shown this by a beautiful experiment, in which he illuminated different portions of a room with

a beam of electric light. Nay, more; we have
good reason to suspect that we are dependent
for the sensation of light, in a great measure, on
the presence of these very dust particles in the
atmosphere. But for their presence, the rays of
light would flow in direct lines, as is the case in
the upper regions of the air, where all is com-
paratively dark except when the observer looks
directly toward the sun. The general diffusion
of light is due to the reflection of the rays in
every direction by these air-motes.

This general view of the subject gives great
interest to the question, "What do we breathe?"
We are no longer confined to the old-fashioned
supposition that if we but avoid certain un-
pleasant conditions, we shall take into our lungs
only pure oxygen and nitrogen, with a little
water vapor. The air we breathe is laden with
impurities. In the air of the streets we inhale
particles of limestone or granite from the pavement and houses; pulverized wood from the
"Nicholson" and the sidewalks; infinitesimal
doses of iron, leather, and textile fabric from
the hoofs of equines and the clothing of our fellows; effete animal matter thrown out from the
lungs of man and brute; excrementitious particles of numerous kinds; constant doses of
sooty matter, and other products of combus-
tion; and remnants of unused food, which are
gathered up by the winds, and distributed "that

nothing may be lost." In the country we may
have less of some of these ingredients, but their
comparative absence is amply supplied by an
excess of vegetable debris. And in both, and
all localities, the air teems with minute vegetable and animal forms of existence, some of
which find there their appropriate sphere, while
others are simply waiting for an opportunity to
develop into larger individualities. It is now
considered to be well ascertained that the
causes of many diseases float about in the
atmosphere, not as inorganic miasmata, as was
formerly supposed, but in the shape of vegetable sporules, or animalcula, which germinate
in the human system under favorable conditions,
after having been received into the lungs in the
act of respiration.

It is more than probable that the philoso-
phers who are investigating the subject have
allowed fear to exaggerate fact to some extent;
yet the general conclusion is undeniable. There
are several forms of epidemic, the transmission
of which can be explained in no other way.
We may instance traumatic (wound) erysipelas,
which is now known to be a fungous growth.
It will often spread through a hospital in a few
hours, though the patients are entirely isolated,
except as they have atmospheric communica-
tion. So with small-pox, which is not simply a
contagion, because it is often extended without

contact. In the former case the vegetable spores are undoubtedly carried by the atmosphere from one wound to another, vegetating externally. In the latter case the poison (probably organic) is carried by the same vehicle, and enters the lungs.

These facts give a key to the philosophy of the simple preventive often resorted to by physicians and nurses in dealing with the sick—placing a handkerchief over the mouth. The *dust* particles are stopped by the woven tissue, while it permits the unladen air to pass to the lungs. There is, however, another fact, which does not seem to be equally well known—the nostrils are provided with an arrangement of little hairs, apparently placed there to fulfil the same end. This system of hairs catches the particles of dust, and allows the air to pass freely. There is no similar protection in the mouth. Hence air respired through the mouth is laden with impurities which can not enter the lungs through the nose. The inference is plain that in exposed situations the mouth should always be kept closed. It is also evident, that, as the air is always more or less loaded with dust, there is continual danger in breathing through the mouth; and, other things being equal, those who sleep with the mouth open will be the most liable to disease.

There is one important fact which seems to

have been altogether lost sight of by those
engaged in this interesting investigation. It is
that the human system, as the systems of all
other organized beings, is built upon a plan
which exactly adapts it to the circumstances
that surround it. Only when some one of the
elements of those circumstances is in excess, or
deficient, either in mass or force, does evil ensue
to the organism. Very many of the substances
which modern investigators have regarded as
hurtful to man, are essential to his existence.
Take carbonic-acid gas, for instance, which is
sent forth from the lungs with every act of
respiration; it is poisonous if mixed with the
atmosphere in more than its usual proportions,
but its presence is absolutely necessary, not
only to the subsistence of plants, and hence to
man indirectly, but directly to him as an essential of his growth. Carbon enters largely into
the human structure, and so does lime, which
appears to be only appropriated by the human
body when presented in the form of a carbonate.
There are those who predict the ultimate extinc-
tion of man from the face of our globe, when
the carbon shall all have been solidified by the
shell-fish and the corals. It is highly probable,
that if the air were purified of all the other matter which is usually regarded as extraneous and
noxious, man would be unable to live in it. Not
only are pure air and pure water (as the term

pure is usually understood) not necessary to a healthy existence, but a certain degree of impurity is one of the conditions of life. We have already noticed that the floating particles of dust are universal light reflectors; and without their aid in diffusing the rays of light, we should soon grow blind, unless the human eye should be found capable of adapting itself to the exigencies imposed by the new condition of things. They undoubtedly have their mission to perform in the lungs; for we can not suppose that they are all strained out in the nostrils. The ciliary arrangement in the nasal apparatus only keeps out that which would be injurious, and allows free access to a normal proportion of the atmospheric burden. Hence we only need to adopt exterior respiratory precautions under conditions of unusual danger. And more than this: we are warranted in assuming that the ordinary use of an artificial respiratory apparatus would work a positive injury, by keeping out of the system some of the elements that are essential to a healthful condition of the frame, which, after all our study, is so little understood.

City life is artificial; but not to the extent which many would have us believe. Man is a gregarious animal, and, except when perverted, has a natural longing for the society of his fellow-beings. The universal harmony of means and ends, which reigns throughout nature, does not warrant us in supposing that our mental longings are normally in a direction contrary to that which instinct would dictate, were it not overshadowed by reason. The atmosphere of a city is not necessarily conducive to short life. There are many occasions on which it is unduly laden with comminuted animal products, but we have already seen that the air of the country is not exempt from its share of the burden, which it seems destined to bear.

The idea that the atmosphere is, or ought to be, composed simply of oxygen and nitrogen, is a delusion; and can only be entertained by one whose views of the constitution of matter are bounded by a very limited horizon. Our earth is an assemblage of material substances, possessing different specific gravities, and endowed also with diverse chemical properties. Without the latter, these substances would long ago have arranged themselves in distinct strata; the heaviest nearest to the centre. Thus we should have in the ascending scale, the metals, then the rocks, perhaps water, and oxygen, nitrogen, and chlorine, hydrogen taking the outer place. But the chemical affinities of all these substances tend to produce a continual union. The double movement of the earth around the sun, and on her own axis, causes perpetual changes in the location of the point of greatest activity of these forces, and the changing position of the moon

causes a continual shifting of the centre of
gravity of the whole mass, and of its constituent parts. As a result of all this, we have an
incessant change of location and form; alternate
formations and disintegrations of inorganic matter, amid which the vital principles of plants and
animals are able to assert a temporary dominion,
by assimilating portions of the vast mass of
moving atoms into forms which are fit theatres
for the display of the vital functions.   And,
"Such is Life."   Liquids circulate among the
solids, and are spread out among the gases.
Solids are taken up in solution by liquids, and
the gases mix and blend, mechanically and
chemically, among themselves, and with all
other forms of matter, the atmosphere being
thus not a distinctive substance, but a mere
emanation from the mass beneath, constantly
interchanging with it, and may be most properly
defined as composed of the lighter and most
minute particles of the various elements, which
make up the sum total of our globe.

Into this material republic, where none, save
the sunbeam, can assert a mastery, the individual man is introduced. He must take this grand
conglomeration of elements as he finds them.
His assimilative powers are exactly adapted to
select from the *melange*, that which is requisite
to the building up of his body; just as the vegetable instincts of the tree and flower enable

them to select the elements which are needed for their nourishment. The more man attempts to doctor the circumstances by which he is surrounded, the greater chance will there be of a speedy inheritance of immortality; and it is only when temporary disturbances of the grand equilibrium arise, that he will benefit himself by bringing his reasoning powers into play. In other words, however repulsive may be the idea of inhaling solid matter at every breath, it is just what we were intended to do; and avoiding precautions are injurious, except under the condition of malarious diseases, or unusual turbulence in the amosphere.

The very same law holds good with the ears, as with the nose. Our aural organs are provided with ciliary appendages, which prevent the introduction of injurious particles. Hence it is worse than useless to clean out the internal part of the ear, and the practice has probably caused more deafness than any other six causes put together. Unless in abnormal conditions of the body, the ear secretes just wax enough for its own uses, and no more. To "clean" it out stimulates the secretion, if it do not absolutely injure the tympanum. Of course all that part of the ear which lies outside the general surface of the head, requires frequent ablution.

As with air, so with water. Medical men have all along told us that the best water for

use is that which is the purest; that is, which
contains the least proportion of other substances
than hydrogen and oxygen. Singularly enough,
it is now a well-established fact that the people
who drink soft water, and those who drink water
which holds the average amount of mineral
matter in solution, die off in the proportion of
13 to 10, other things being equal.

Truth is always consistent with itself; and
science is the knowledge of truth. The great
end of science is a knowledge of the truth about
ourselves; which involves a cognizance of our
relations to surrounding objects, and hence to
the whole universe. The basis of much of this
science rests on the apparently very unstable
foundation of "what we breathe."

THE FIRST CHRISTMAS-EVE.

1878 YEARS BEFORE A.D. 1874.

———

MANY centuries ago, long before the ruthless
hand of science had snatched away the golden
chain which linked the angels and the stars
with men, in daily communion,

> When time was young,
> And birds conversed as well as sung;
> And gift of speech was not confined
> Merely to brutes of human kind,

the whole creation, since reduced by modern
philosophy to an innumerable assemblage of
masses of inanimate matter, dotted, here and
there, with specks of thinking organism, was
instinct with life. Man was not, then, the sole
entity of intelligent existence in the visible universe. The beasts of the field and forest held
parliamentary sessions. The birds of the air
met in joyous conclave to discourse their
thoughts to each other. The denizens of the
briny deep claimed oral affinity with their

brethren of the land. The insect world thought
aloud; and even the trees and the grasses were
endowed with the power of speech. Still, man
was the most highly favored of them all. The
angels came down in the daytime, and talked
with him; while at night the stars twinkled
responsively to his salutations, and pointed out
to him his destiny as they slowly wandered
through the heavens. There was sin in the
world, and "death by sin," for primeval innocence no longer existed. But the harmony of
nature had not been disturbed by the iconoclast
of to-day. The morning stars sang together,
without fear of modern criticism, while the Sons
of God "shouted aloud for joy"; and the
refrain was taken up in gladsome chorus by the
inhabitants of earth, the whole creation joining
in a vocal anthem in praise of its Creator.

Years rolled by. Other years followed in
their train, and yet more; the gloom cast o'er
the face of Nature by "man's first disobedience,
and the fruit of that forbidden tree" deepening
with the flight of centuries. Gradually the
angels withdrew from the walks of men. The
stars grew more "distant," shrinking from famil-
iarity with the growing corruption of the human
race; and the lower animals became dumb with
astonishment at the conduct of their representa-
tives in the court of the higher intelligences. A
night of thick darkness had settled down upon

the descendants of Adam; their accumulated
wickedness cried to Heaven as the blood of
Abel. A fate seemed to be impending, bitter
as that which befell the inhabitants of Sodom
and Gomorrah—universal as that which over-
took the world in the days of Noah.

———

It was a lovely night, near midwinter, 1878
years ago, as the sun touched the lowest point
in his southward trend, before rising again
toward the summit of the heavens, when Nature
was roused from her slumbers to witness and
take part in an event which formed a third
epoch in the history of the world. No tocsin
gave warning of an occurrence equally memor-
able with the creation of our own globe; but
the news was mysteriously conveyed to every
part of the universe. From the bright shining
stars to the least particle of matter that forms
a molecule on this earth, all were wakened up
into new life; all partook of an excitement not
paralleled since the ultimate atoms first began
to gather together to form chemical elements
and then worlds.

A little spot in the beautiful land of Palestine
was the centre of an attraction, equally wonderful, and not less mighty, than that which causes
the ponderous Jupiter to revolve around the
sun. The birds of the air came flocking to-

gether, attracted by the mysterious influence, which they seemed to recognize, if they could not understand. The beasts of the field gathered from afar, in lessening circles, and went down on their knees in solemn reverence. Even the animals that prey seemed to forget their instinctive desire to devour, and stood trans-fixed with silent awe. The clouds which had gathered early in the evening slowly disappeared as midnight approached, melting away into nothingness through the ethereal vault; and the very face of nature was changed, the grass springing up, and the trees blossoming anew as when the summer draweth nigh.

The earth was canopied by the most brilliant of the starry host, and from the northwest to the southern quarter of the heavens stretched the milky stream of starlight that once formed the pathway along which angels passed on their errands between man and the throne of the Eternal. Only two of the then-known planets were above the horizon. The moon was nearing the end of her last quarter, following the beautiful Venus, which, about the time that the first gray streaks of dawn were visible in the eastern sky, would rise as Phosphor, or "Lucifer, the son of the morning," heralding the approach of the sun. Mars had already sunk in the west, and the winged-heeled Mercury was near the Nadir, dancing attendance upon Apollo in the stellar

Hades. The giant Jupiter, with his little family of worlds, had recently passed near the zenith, and his light rivaled that of the mighty Sirius; both far outshining the jewels in the Belt of Orion, which were nearly equidistant from those two resplendent orbs. Jupiter was preceded by his elder brother, Saturn, whose paler light was scarcely less bountifully dispensed to the inhabitants of earth, as he ticked off the flight of time at the rate of one year for each day in the lunar circuit,—a labor which had long before gained for him the title of "Chronos."

Suddenly the heavenly vault itself seemed to be quickened into a new life; expanding into the forms that had been assigned by the earlier sages, which changed their attitudes into unison with the scene below. The Lamb (the Ram of our present Zodiac), sinking peacefully to rest in the bosom of night, aroused itself at once to take part in the solemn pageant. Cassiopea looked up from her throne, and the shackles fell from the limbs of Andromeda at the touch of her deliverer. The Bull ceased his threatening attitude toward the monster Orion; who, in return, dropped his club, and lifted his foot from the neck of the Hare, which he had trampled into submission for untold ages. The Bears, high up in the northeastern regions, paused in their journey around the Pole (to escape the bite of the howling dogs, and the lash of the venge-

ful Herdsman), and looked down upon the scene
with equal interest; while the hounds themselves, as if wearied with the chase, turned to
gaze in mute adoration. The Wagoner rested
in his attempt to lasso the Twins, who twined
still more closely in their loving embrace. The
Lion, toiling rapidly up the steep ascent toward
the fervid heats of the mid-heaven, no longer
roared defiance to the rest of the heavenly host,
but bent submissively, as if charmed for awhile
into pristine innocence by the majesty of the
scene. The Raven ceased its croaking, and the
Snake withdrew its forked tongue, as if it, too,
would be at peace with earth and Heaven.
The Greater Dog, stern but faithful guardian of
the Nile, who had heralded the rising of its
mighty waters many centuries before the pyra-
mids were built, or the Sphynx put forth its
riddles, assumed a look of unwonted benevo-
lence. The Virgin, coming up from the East
with a sparkling brilliant in her hand, shining
resplendent, like Venus rising from the sea-
foam, was bathed in beauty, glittering in all
the purity of maidenhood.

Gradually the sun neared the lowest point in
his diurnal circuit. As he touched the nether
meridian, the constellations themselves gave
way, and broke up in the glow of light from
their component gems. Every member of the
stellar universe was again individualized; but

only that each star, shining brightly in the
cloudless sky, might be transformed from a
speck of light to a living being. Their scintil-
lating rays assumed the shape of pinions, on
which the celestial messengers of the Eternal
winged their way through space. The majestic
Sirius, brightest of all the stars, and prince of
the firmament in the absence of the god of day,
seemed like the archangel, whose effulgence out-
shines that of the ordinary seraph, as the sun
pales the moon when in her presence. The
valiant Procyon followed in his train. The
mighty Arcturus, "with his sons," pointed toward the throne around which clustered the cher-
ubim, as they winged their flight toward the
earth. The beauteous Capella took up her kids
to do honor to the occasion. Castor and Pollux
suspended their arrangement to be immortal
by turns, and moved together in a harmonious
blaze of glory. The maimed hand (Chaph)
assumed a female form that beckoned to a
celestial Elysium. The "Basiliskos" (cor Leon-
is) appeared as the Lion of the Tribe of Judah
from whose loins should spring the Lord's
Anointed One; while Aldebaran led the way.
Only one of the prominent stars in the visible
heavens failed to join in the great transforma-
tion; the Demon Star, in the head of the
Gorgon, retreated behind its gaseous satellite,
as if ashamed to appear in a physical aspect

not in harmony with the rest. It was a concourse of stars, of angels, of men; that seemed
to be gathered with a common object,—uniting
for some common purpose, that should be
fraught with untold happiness to the inhabitants of earth.

Amid this unwonted display, the two greater
planets had moved silently and steadily, though
swiftly forward, seeming to take no heed of the
general transfiguration. Now the radiance of
Jupiter took on the form of the god whose
thunders had shaken Olympus in the hoary
past. But his hand no longer held the bolts
before which heaven had so often quailed; it
now grasped the trident of Neptune, the symbol
of a mysterious Trinity, soon to be revealed to
the world. Then, even Old Father Chronos
paused in his tireless flight, and, from his position on the prime vertical over the western horizon, waved his hour-glass as a signal that the
culminating act in the drama should begin. As
he did so his features seemed to change from
the rugosity of age, back to the juvenile freshness they exhibited when he set forth on his
travels at the dawn of creation. The phenome-
non was a fit accompaniment to the beginning
of a new era; the year "one" no longer dating
from the time when the breath of life was
breathed into the nostrils of Adam by the *Elo-
him*. The signal was responded to by six of

the seven daughters of Atlas, the Pleiades, who
moved eastward to the zenith. Since then the
seventh has been invisible to mortal eye, her
brightness being dimmed by the act of disobedience, as Adam lost his corona of light when
he fell. These six, the Western Atlantides,
more favored than their sister Hyades, wended
their flight toward the Crab, in mid-heaven.
From out its shining depths they culled the
Cradle nebula, which, studded with living jewels,
between two milk-white asses, was born by them
downward, and to the spot where the worshipers
of earth had gathered in reverential attitude.
As the gorgeous procession neared the ground,
a tiny human form appeared within the burden,
and the very air seemed to be warmed as by the
breath of Omnipotence. Then the angelic forms
assumed by the stars in the Belt of Orion, which
had "come up from the East" during the evening, approached as three kings, their flowing
beards and talismanic-covered garments pro-
claiming them as belonging to the *Magi.* They
bore rich offerings in their hands, which they
laid at the feet of the little stranger. The first
a purse of gold, the offering of earth-dross to
the heaven-born one. The second, a gift of
precious stones, brighter than any that adorned
the crown of Solomon or the breastplate of the
High Priest of Israel in the days when God answered his chosen people by Urim and Thum-

mim. The third offered rich spices, whose per-
fumes, filling the air, were emblematic of kingly
adoration in life, and also of preservation in
death. As they drew around the infant form,
the earth-born ones chorused forth a joyous anthem, which was taken up by the whole host of
heaven, and chanted in every part of the universe, "Peace on earth, good-will to men."

————

The morning twilight dawned upon a world in
slumbers. The stars had resumed their places
in the firmament, and their light rapidly faded
before that of the approaching sun. No trace
remained of the midnight pomp; except a baby,
"wrapped in swaddling-clothes and lying in a
manger," near which was grouped a party of
shepherds, who had left their flocks reposing in
the neighboring fields while they went to see
what had caused the unparalleled commotion of
the previous night.

Unparalled afterward, as before! The history of that night was too grand to be repeated.
A tradition existed, for many centuries afterward, that on each return of the anniversary of
that concourse, the cattle on a thousand hills
repeated the obeisance then tendered Him to
whom every knee should bow. But even that
homage is no longer paid. The cold facts of a
Gradgrind-world are not now disturbed by best-

ial deference or devotion, still less by celestial interference in the affairs of men. The stars have ceased to be personal, though they yet teach general truths to those who interrogate them aright; and nature no longer speaks, except in that still, small voice, in which the Prophet Elijah heard more than was told in the whirlwind and the storm. But the events of that night have formed the warp of all subsequent history, the woof to which has been gradually filled in by man in succeeding generations. Not until the angel stand with one foot on the sea and the other upon the earth, and swear by Him that liveth forever that there shall be time no longer, will that mighty web be finished. Nor will it be unraveled in eternity. The peace then declared between man and his Creator, sealed by the blood of the Holy One, and ratified by the deaths of countless thousands of martyrs, is a bond between Earth and Heaven that may never be broken. It is a peace which passeth all understanding; and, like the Word of the Lord, then given, endureth forever.

[NOTE.—There are good reasons for placing the Birth of Christ four years earlier than the date assigned by the Christian era. The writer also wishes to disarm hostile criticism by admitting that the "Hunting Dogs" are not in the list of constellations enumerated by Ptolemy. If any one still objects that they ought not to have been introduced, or that the Magian gifts have been misrepresented, he, or she, is commended to the Apology of Phædrus,— "*delectamus fictis fabulis.*"]

THE SUN THAT NEVER SETS.

1732–1879.

———

I WAS informed last Monday evening that I should be called upon to speak to this topic, and have prepared myself accordingly; like the boy who backed himself with three or four thicknesses of carpeting when told to prepare for a whipping. My first idea was that you expect from me a learned essay on solar physics, which should begin *ab initio*, like Jenkinson in "The Vicar of Wakefield", and carry you down to the time when Macauley's New Zealander will lament the destruction of our big telescope. But, on second thoughts, I remind myself, as a Frenchman might say, that astronomy is my pet weakness; and have determined not to follow the example of the man who could never— that is, almost never—talk for three minutes without dragging his little bay pony in by the ears. I have decided to gratify my taste for unnatural history by changing the U into an O, though I run the risk of breaking Grimm's law into a thousand pieces.

We need not long follow the modern method
of hunting down, to find our subject; though we
may not be able to recognize him by the hay
on his horns. The son referred to necessarily
belongs to the ovipara; since the act and fact of
setting is absurd where there are no eggs—unless, indeed, we except the setter-dog of the
sportsman, who "set by the fire" when satisfied;
and Sheridan's oyster, which could not be a fine
native because it was a settler. Our research,
then, rapidly bears down upon that department
of natural history known as ornithology; and—
well, the joke is so tame that we may regard it
as fairly domesticated.

I confess that the day, or rather the morrow,
suggests the eagle; that proud bird of freedom
which, at the bidding of our friend Harrison,
flaps his wings all over this broad continent in
less time than it took Logan to master the
financial question. I might say that the time
referred to was a fortnight, but am afraid the
joke would be two week to be of value. The
eagle enjoys the proud distinction of having his
pinions plumed for a flight into the eye of the
sun, by the immortal George Washington—I
was tempted to say the talon-ted Washington,
but will not say it, and beg the pardon of the
District of Columbia for having even thought
of such a half-fledged pun. A great deal more
might be said in favor of the eagle, if I could

only think of it; but I candidly confess that I do not like the eagle, except when on a piece of gold, and will not further eulogize him—nor his son. I can not forget that one of the nations of Europe flaunts a $20 gold piece—I mean a double eagle—in the eyes of the world; and I hate duplicity—even in a star. I do not believe in seeing things double, not even a *double-enten-dre*. It is a reflection on the red-ribbon movement, which I heartily endorse—I mean the movement, not the reflection.

It is the never setting son of the hen that merits *my* praise. The rooster is king! He may not be the Alpha of creation, but he is certainly the Omega—if Sir Walter Scott is to be credited, and like the immortal George, he never told a lie. You all know to what I refer:—his eloquent description of "The Lay of the Last Minstrel."

Let me ask you—but no, I will ask myself, this not being a class-room—where would Καισορ have been without his Transalpine Gallus? and how much would your classic history amount to without Cæsar? Once more, and this time by particular request, as they say in the advertising columns of the *Tribune*, where now would be the glorious Union, for which Washington so gloriously fought, but for Grant? and is not Grant a son of Gallina? Still again, and this positively the last, what is the goose as com-

pared with the rooster, in the history of Rome?
Anser me if you can.

I am proud of the fact that Washington and
the rooster, between them, have solved one of
the biggest problems that ever taxed the ener-
gies of a mental philosopher; in his senior year.
The question—which was created first, the hen
or the egg?—was triumphantly answered a few
years before Washington sought in vain for a
Pons Asinorum, over which he might cross the
Delaware. The egg of freedom was first made,
and the boy George was raised up to hatch-it.
And thus liberty was born; though more than
half a century elapsed before its head was entirely freed from the shell. I am more than
half-inclined to believe that the cherry-tree is
as much of a myth as was the writing of his
own plays by Shakespeare. It seems to have
been put into the story by some one who did
not comprehend the true inwardness of the fact;
and for that reason the commentators have
barked around it for the best part of a century,
in the fruitless effort to obtain uncommon taters
by digging away at the root of the tree of
liberty.

To me the moral of the story is plainly on
the exterior. If George had really wanted to
cut down that tree he would have done it; and
if he only wished to try the temper of his
hatchet, as well as that of his father, he would

have selected sterner stuff. His biographers had been more *liber*-al if less litter-al in descriptively strewing the garden with chips. There was evidently but one chip in the case; and Washington senior recognized it as having been chopped from the old block. All else is purely fanciful—unless it be etymological. I incline to take the latter view. The *liber cérasi*, which I will not insult your intelligence by saying is Choctaw for "the bark of the cherry-tree", seems to have become the *liber* tree, which was corrupted into liberty—as liberty itself was corrupted into license when the painter of the picture capped the climax of absurdity by supposing its leading feature to be a cap. Any electrician of today can tell you that the Gessler cap—the original of the idea—was only a Geissler tube, borrowed from Switzerland. Hence, if it be a piece of head-gear at all, it must be of the stovepipe order of architecture.

I tell you, Washington was a grand man; though I believe he never rose to the dignity of being a grand father—as so many of you have done. I will yield to no man in my admiration of his over-towering greatness, which will be remembered long after the best of us has been forgotten. *That* grandeur is one of the few human suns that never set. And he is especially entitled to admiration because he achieved magnificent results with small means.

You know it is proverbial that the best work-
man is always the one who can work with the
poorest materials and the fewest tools. The
professor, for instance, who can fill a cabbage-
head with Greek roots, or cultivate it up to a
masterly knowledge of surds, deserves to rank
high among his Fellows—or among other men,
if there be no Fellowships in his University.
Now, Washington made a cherry-tree immortal,
and a nation free. He hewed out for himself a
niche high up in the temple of fame, burst
asunder the yoke of tyranny which had so long
galled the necks of the American people, and
cut down the prejudices of Europe against the
principle and the practice of popular govern-
ment. How grandly simple were the means he
employed—the tool with which he worked! He
did it with his little hatchet! He did! for he
told us so himself; or rather he told his father;
and it must be true, because he could not tell a
lie. We have his own word for that, and he
was certainly a much better authority than
Mark Twain, who *could* tell a lie, but would n't.
Give *me* the boy who *can not* lie, and says so
himself—when a Freshman. Such a one will be
a jewel when a Sophomore—albeit despised like
Æsop's jewel on the dunghill. He will have
developed into a *rara-avis* by the time he is a
Junior; and will become an angel in his Senior
year, fit to graduate into paradise.

If I were only a Joshua, who could make the
sun abstain from setting, I might be able to say
something, in conclusion, to the subject you
have given me. But I am not. I do not even
know an instance in which any one of the millions of suns that dot the firmament does not
rise, and set, to its attendant family of worlds.
It is probable that every planet in existence has
one point in common with the Celtic policeman
who slowly made his way along the gutter
because he was too *spirited* to use the sidewalk:
—he was described as "Pat-rolling on his axis."
I went a long way out West last summer toward
the place where the sun sets, but was no nearer
to the non-setting point than if I had stayed at
home. My journey, in that respect, was about
equally bootless with that of the

> —— bumpkin who had oft been told
> The story of the pot of gold,
> Which fame reports is to be found
> Just where the rainbow meets the ground.

Permit me to hint, however, that where I
have failed, others may be more successful. On
this earth, no; but measurably so on our attendant moon. Keeping nearly the same side always
toward us, the good people there, if any there
be, on the hither side, will always have the
earth above their horizon; and during a part of
every month our globe will give to them nearly
as much light as is received from the sun by

the inhabitants of Neptune, the most distant known planet in the solar system. The result, however, is disastrous in the extreme, in a scientific respect. The earth-shine during their solar night is so intense that, with an atmosphere sufficiently dense to permit the existence of air-breathing beings, the lunarians are cut off from studying the stars—except a few of the brightest. We have good reason to believe that the moon was once inhabited, and that she probably is now a died-out world. The foregoing reasoning then must apply to the past, instead of the present. The Lunar habitants of a great many centuries ago could scarcely have been astronomers, as we understand the meaning of the word. To make the word fit them, we should have to change the order of the letters, and let it read "Moon-starers".

Let me add that, so far as we can reason on the subject, we should be in the same plight now if we were blessed, or cursed, with a never-setting sun. The alternation of night with day is not only a merciful provision for the recuperation of exhausted Nature, but a wonderful aid to our knowledge; as without it we should scarcely be aware of the existence of any world outside our own. As Uriah Heep might have remarked, we have much to be thankful for; and among those things is the fact that our search for knowledge is not hampered by the presence of a "sun that never sets."

www.ingramcontent.com/pod-product-compliance
Lightning Source LLC
Chambersburg PA
CBHW021246260626
47172CB00002B/866